NIGHT STAGE

Mystery Chapter Series Volume 1

By Nesi Jordan

"Never forget that Justice is what
Love looks like in public."
~Cornel West

"Every night, it's a different stage, a place where strange things occur. It's our job to catch these vultures, especially on the internet. It's a must to continue to spread knowledge and get justice for sex trafficking and internet predatory."
~Survivors

Table of Contents

Chapter 1

THE CHANGE-UP

Leading officers that just got off their last shift rush down the police department hallway before they receive their merits joking around. Macy Pierce strolled with a funky attitude, not expecting her partner Ryan Pullah to leave the division. He's transferring to sunny Florida. Ryan starts limping in pain and says to Macy, "Well, looks like you finally got what you wanted." Macy smiles. "Yeah. Wait a minute, we both did". Ryan took a step back and said to Macy, "Naw, today is my last day." Macy looked surprised and said, "Ryan, what the hell are you talking about? "What do you mean, your last day?

Ryan took a step back, looked at Macy again, and said, "I'm getting too old for this shit; my leg is dragging now, My wife is missing family vacations, and you don't listen to a damn word I say! "You gotta learn, Macy; when you have a partner, you have to work as a team. Macy took a hard stare at Ryan and yelled, "I do work as a team." Ryan paused and undecidedly looked toward Macy and said, "Not all the time." Macy yelled out loud, "What the hell does that suppose to mean?"

Chief Lambert opens her office door and greets Macy and Ryan with a smile. Pullah tapped Macy on the shoulder and whispered in her ear; "You'll find out". Chief Lambert shuts her office door and grabs a piece of paper off her desk and says " Pullah and Pierce front and center". Macy looked at Ryan and mumbled under her breath "Shit I thought today was a special day." Ryan says with a haunting stare to Macy "It is. My last day".

Macy stands in place biting the inside of her mouth with a nasty disposition thinking about Ryan leaving and who's going to be her partner. Chief Lambert breaks the ice by saying "Congratulations on becoming detectives, Unfortunately, Pullah you're departing us and transferring to. Ryan tried to stop Chief Lambert from saying the transfer, Ryan wanted her to say retire. Chief Lambert cleared her throat and finished her announcement in a stern voice "To Florida, Lucky You!"

Macy turned to Ryan with a disgusted look on her face and said "Florida. I thought yo Ass was leaving the force because you were too old, Your leg is starting to drag and your wife misses family vacations? Ryan cuts off Macy and says sarcastically" And you don't listen to a damn word I say". Macy gets right in Ryan's face and raises her voice and says "What! you know what Ryan. '' Chief Lambert came between the officers and looked and said, "Detective Pierce stop whining, We have more serious issues at hand."

Macy sighed and mumbled under her breath "You know what." Chief Lambert looked Macy in her eyes and replied " What, Do they work here? I don't care how you feel right now Pierce, Pullah is transferring and that's it. Detective Pullah here's your papers and have a safe trip. Ryan grabs his papers from Chief Lambert and says "Thank You". leans toward Macy and puts his sunglasses on and whispers "I'll send you a postcard." Chief Lambert's office phone starts ringing and Macy shakes her head with attitude and mumbled "Boy I tell ya,Folks Lie so much these days".

Chief Lambert told her assistant on the phone to send in her next appointment. Macy was still in disbelief about Ryan transferring; Chief Lambert paused and said, "Detective Pierce since Pullah is no longer here, I've assigned you to another partner". Macy stood up and responded " Awe Chief, Now you realize that there's no one in this division that could work with me, they all get on my damn nerves. They either are too old or dingy as hell. I could just ride solo for a couple of months."

Chief Lambert's office door opens and Macy's new partner walks in. Macy jumps up and yells " Oh Hell No! Chief Lambert formally acquaints Detroit's own Detective Macy Pierce. Meet your new partner Tennessee's finest Detective, Naomi Barker. Now if you all would excuse me; I have some papers I have to look over; here are your first tasks. Here you go,

Detective". Naomi stretched out her hand to greet Macy, and she looked at Naomi, nudged her, and fumed out of Chief Lambert's office.

Detective Naomi Barker grabs the assignments and says," Thank you, Ma'am, in her southern belle accent. Naomi leaves out of Chief Lambert's office as the Chief gets on the phone and asks for her assistant to send officer Chez in her office. Naomi spots Macy jumping in her vehicle, and Naomi rushes over to give her the assignment sheet for their next task. Detective Barker knocks on Macy's window, saying in her southern belle accent," Didn't you forget something? Macy snatches the paper and speeds off. Naomi coughs and says in a bitter voice," Your welcome." Naomi glanced at the assignment sheet and noticed Macy's phone number, and started walking towards the U Haul truck where her husband was awaiting her return.

Chapter 2

SPICY MOUTH FROM THE SOUTH

Detective Naomi Barker decided to call Detective Macy Pierce's cell number off her assignment sheet. The phone rang twice, and Macy answered with a puzzled voice," hello? On the other end of the phone, Macy heard a southern voice respond," Hey Detective! Remember me? Macy was perplexed and asked," Who is this? The southern voice answered," Naomi." At that moment, Macy was trying to disregard and replied," Naomi, who? Naomi took a deep breath and said," Your partner." Macy gave a smart-mouth comment saying," My partner left…He's in Florida".

Naomi replied in a stern voice, " Look, detective! I know you don't like this new arrangement. Still, we have a task to do, and I thought you had a little class to put aside this kiddie bullshit and let's work on this extreme case, Macy; you're so used to telling others what to do you forget about the team". Macy cutoff Naomi and replied, "First of all, country bumpkin. You don't know me and don't you ever call this phone line again; When we see and talk to each other, it will be at work; Other than that, don't call here again. Did you get that?

Naomi looked at the phone and proceeded to speak with authority and replied, " Get this, Detective, you don't scare me, whatsoever! I'm here to do a job, and that's what I'm going to fulfill; as for the country bumpkin, Search this southern belle's records. You have a good night, Detective,". And Naomi hangs up the phone. Macy, later on, took Naomi's advice, got on the computer, and searched her records; Macy sighed and said, " Why the hell is she here? Hmmm, interesting. Macy found out Naomi Barker was Raised in foster care with three other siblings that were abandoned at the age of five after a firebomb initiated by her foster mom; Naomi went on to her foster mother oldest sister, that was a veteran of the Military and was raised with her cousins that were all into criminal law enforcement and legal experts that were a dream one day Naomi wanted to accomplish. Macy kept scrolling and noticed Detective Naomi Barker graduated from field academy; top of her sharpshooting class, had a nervous breakdown because the other classmates didn't want to work with her, so she started going to therapy and decided to transfer to another division.

Macy starts scrolling down on the computer in awe, and her child walks in the room asking for a glass of chocolate milk. Macy was startled and said, " Baby, what are you doing up? The child started wiping their eyes and replied: " I'm thirsty." Macy took the child to the kitchen to get a glass of water and sent the child off to bed. Macy turned her computer off, Blew out her scented candle, and got in the bed.

Chapter 3

UNBOXED MEMOIRS

Later on, that night, detective Naomi Barker started working on her Assignment sheet; with so much clutter of unopened boxes from the move, she didn't waste any time. Naomi searched on her computer, taking a sip of an ice-cold beer while listening to her southern blues. Naomi starts mumbling," I've seen too many cases like this…just sick". Naomi's husband Stanley Barker of five years agreed to change positions after her treatment sessions from her last job; Naomi has known Stanley for almost fifteen years. They met during a Tennessee stakeout after Stanley loss his wife of two years to breast cancer, and they never disconnected.

Stanley started looking around for the clean towels and walked into the living room and kissed Naomi on the cheek and said in a southern accent," Naomi hun, you gotta get some rest; We still got to unpack; where are the towels? I need to do a quick shave". Naomi was still looking on the computer, not hearing a word, Stanley just said. Naomi mumbled to herself while scrolling on the computer," This 25-year-old guy set up a date with a 16-year-old girl; he posted that he was 17 years old and needed a date for the senior prom; just deceiving!

Stanley called Naomi again frustratedly," Naomi Hun, where's the linen box." Naomi responded irritatedly," Babe, I put the towels away." Stanley checked in the hall cabinet, shook his head, and mumbled," now she tells me." Stanley starts shaving, and Naomi turns off the computer and starts cutting open boxes, putting her awards away reminiscing on her accomplishments. Stanley comes out of the restroom all fresh-faced and trim, hugs and kisses Naomi speaking in her ear," Naomi hun, Let's hit the sack…You and I need some rest; it's already midnight". Naomi turned

7

toward Stanley and gently rubbed his face, and replied:" I have five more to put away, and I promise suga muffin; I'm coming to bed." Stanley kissed Naomi's hand and whispered ``goodnight." Naomi drank the last of her cold beer and finished placing her awards in the curio with pride.

Chapter 4

RANK ALERT

This early morning is the day all of the new and old detectives have a meeting in Chief Lambert's office, discussing a case on Internet predators; Macy struts in, and the whole room was complete except for one seat that was right next to Naomi, and of course, Macy didn't like that. A pleasant voice echoed," Good morning! Welcome back to the old, and Congratulations to our new ranks as detectives; we have secondary training." declares Chief Lambert.

Macy looks around and insists on walking past an empty chair; Chief Lambert calls her out as she points to the open seat and says," Morning, detective Pierce. So lovely of you to join us, Have a seat". Macy completely ignores Naomi smiling and trying to say morning to Macy. Chief Lambert brought out a chalkboard and stated:" Before we go out into the field, we are going to do some team building. I have a list that I assigned groups".

Macy hits the desk with anger, and Chief Lambert asks Macy if there is a problem? Macy responded rapidly," Yeah, What's the point? Chief Lambert replied in a stern voice, " The point is to test your strengths and weaknesses." Macy says with a nasty disposition," My strengths and weaknesses are just fine." Chief Lambert glared and responded to Macy and said:" Detective, your shortcoming is working as a team." The whole class was in shock. Chief Lambert continued to share with the group and stated that she put together training scenarios and had their uniforms; she called out Team one Dutton, Ramiez, Berts, and Patton. Team two Jordan, Lakewood, Charles, and Brown. Team three Bradford, Chase, Pierce, and Barker.

Chief Lambert stated she finds working as a group can get better results. Music started to play as each group set up for the target practice; Center massed both high scores for 280-300; the Range officers tallied up the points and stated," Good job, ladies! Naomi says," Thanks! And Macy high five him and says," Thank you, Robbie! The range officer smiled and asked whether the ladies would celebrate tonight. Macy frowned and responded," We're sure not."

Naomi chuckles and says to Macy," Awww! Come on, detective, we deserve it. Let's get a beer". Macy replied," I don't drink beer. Naomi gets truly excited and belts out," Well, a Cosmo/ Margarita. Whatever you want, I'm buying." The Range officer says in a chipper voice," Can I go? Naomi says in a sharp mood as she walks away," If you want... Not my treat, though". The range officer responded embarrassingly," ooooh, Alrighty then." Naomi and Macy sashayed out the door and waved goodbye.

Chapter 5

CELEBRATE TRUTH

Inside Bernie Ray's Country Bar, Detective Naomi Barker's husband Stanley works as a part-time bartender manager; A group of people line dancing in the middle of the floor having a blast of fun. Here Naomi and Macy look around, and Naomi rushes over to the bartender and says," Hey baby, Let me get two-night beers and for the Lil lady a cosmo." Macy frowns her face and replies," A cosmo?

Stanley, the bartender, swings his towel in the air and whispers' ' Two night-beers and a cosmo.... Hey darling, can I take you home tonight? Naomi flirted back with Stanley and pulled him close, and said seductively," You sure can, babe." Stanley replies in excitement," I get off in 20 minutes". Macy's eyes bucked in disbelief while Naomi winked at Stanley and said, "Okay, hun." Macy grabbed her cosmo drink and said sarcastically," You southern belles don't waste any time." Naomi put down her beer, smirked, and confessed:" That's my husband sherlock." Macy gave herself a facepalm and quickly apologized and replied " Sorry... Why did you ask me to come here?

Naomi was brutally honest by saying," I needed a ride, and I wanted to celebrate today's success.....Look here, Macy, I don't want us to have any ill feelings toward one another, and I know you enjoy your space. It's your right to be protective overall, But detective, we will kick major ass together in these cases". Macy stands up and raises her cosmo glass and replies," I want to get these scumbags off the street...Do we have a deal? Naomi raised her eyebrows and picked up her beer bottle, and shouted," Hell yeah, it's a deal! Macy was anxious and said," Where do you want to start?

Naomi dug in her pouch and grabbed her highlighted paper with numerous groups she researched last night and shared with Macy. Naomi says," I guess we could start signing up with some online teen sites and get these internet predators locked up; Detective, we have two weeks to find these freak parties." Macy and Naomi looked at each other and said at the same urgency," And Bust Them All! Macy blurted out," I read the other night that this sixteen-year girl was asked to attend a senior prom and was raped; her mother found her middle finger in a plastic bag with a note saying," She got fucked! Macy shook her head and said," Just a damn shame."

Naomi was so disgusted she replied: " Wow! This has to stop. In the morning, I'll bring some alias names and passwords. Every party we are invited to, let's go and bust their asses. Stanley interrupted the conversation and said to Naomi, `` Excuse me, alright hun, let's roll out here". Naomi grabbed Stanley's hand. She said," Stanley, baby, l want to introduce you to my new partner, detective Macy Pierce. My husband, Stanley Barker ". Macy reached out her hand, and Naomi nudged Stanley, and he blurted out," I'm so sorry. Nice to finally meet you, detective; I've heard a lot about you". Naomi clears her throat, and Macy responds," That's okay. I admit I was a bitch, but we have an excellent right partner? Naomi grabbed Macy's hand with a tear in her eye and said," Right partner."

Stanley didn't want to interrupt their bond, but he placed his hand on Naomi's waist and said:" Okay, detectives, we gotta go. I'm drained. Nice meeting you again, Macy." Naomi starts walking away, and Macy says," It was a pleasure. Hey detective Barker, good score today at the range, I thought I was the only badass, But you did yo thang." Naomi blushed and answered back," Thanks a lot, Detective; I appreciate that; See you in the morning! As Naomi started strolling towards the door, Macy waved goodbye.

Chapter 6

PLAN INVITED

Unusual eyes are gawking at the screen surfacing the Internet, loud clicking at the keyboard trying to allure underage girls; the vultures are back on the prowl. The predator created a strategy and sent a few invites for his next prey; while It's trouble down at the precinct with an older white woman asking the officers for a match, the officers responded:" You can't smoke in here, ma'am." The older woman replied," I don't want to smoke. I Want to burn this place down to the ground". The officers instantly locked her up for a premeditated ordinance.

Chief Lambert started shouting at Macy and Naomi about what was going on before they arrived. She began to let them know that an older lady threatened to burn down the police station, and Macy yelled in shock "What! Are you kidding me? Chief Lambert replied "Yes! Her cat was stuck in a tree and she claimed the officers took too long getting there so her cat was starving to death." Naomi says " I'm so glad we missed that live entertainment".

Chief Lambert logged into her laptop and says" Speaking of entertainment, We need to find these freak parties and start busting them up, But I need you both to speed up your investigation". Macy stood up and stretched and Chief Lambert stood up and started in a stern voice " Detective Pierce…Don't start with your feisty disposition either". Macy started smirking and answered back " We are good over here Chief ". Naomi chimes in and states "Yeah the beef is squashed".

Chief Lambert sat back down in her office chair and replied" Good… What information do you have so far? Naomi speaks clearly and says " Well Chief, we noticed one guy comes online around 9:30 pm until 11 pm… I chatted for an hour and he invited me to a red underwear party; I thought that was strange". Macy pulled out her highlighted observations and stated:" I monitored a guy that's looking for a girl with braces, He says he likes to feel pain". Chief Lambert put her hands on her head with a look of disgust and said " Sicko...Just a hot mess".

Naomi chimes in to share her notes and says " I was invited to a party on Saturday, This guy was very nice…He looks kinda nerdy though". Macy concurs and says " Those are the ones you have to keep an eye on. I got the same email; it's ``fill the glass gathering; bring your glasses and just talk, it's a geek freak party". Chief Lambert replies "It's weird but maybe you both need to check it out". Macy hopped right on her laptop and accepted the invite, and said," Let The party begin!

Chapter 7

MIXED MESSAGES

Early Saturday morning Chief Lambert fulfilled her typical routine checking her email, finishing her ginger flavor tea, and clasping her sweater while walking outside to check her mailbox. Chief Lambert read her letter out of the mailbox and noticed it read her neighbor's address. Chief Lambert grumbled, "What in the world is this? Soon as Chief Lambert looked up, she heard a soft voice from across the street and noticed it was her neighbor Lil Rita strolling towards her,

Chief Lambert's only son Brian watched out the upstairs window while Lil Rita presented Chief Lambert with her mail, saying, "Hey Miss Lambert, I gotcha mail by mistake. Chief Lambert exchanged the mail and replied, " I swear this mail lady needs to be fired. Hey Rita, How are you? Lil Rita said in a chipper voice, " I'm good; I just passed my driver's training test." Chief Lambert shut her mailbox and said, " Oh yeah. Wait a minute; you're sixteen now? Wow, I remember when you were helping your grandma plant flowers in the yard having summer tea parties with your baby dolls.

Lil Rita smiled and said, " I turned sixteen yesterday, and my big mama surprised me with a new car; I was so excited. Chief Lambert said, " Happy Belated Birthday honey, drive safely and be cautious with these parties; These men are luring these young girls and attacking them. Be a very cautious sweetie and tell your big mama I said hello, and I'm looking forward to that bowl of chicken gumbo she promised me.

Lil Rita said at a distance, " Ok, I will. Thank you!

As Chief Lambert was walking in the house reading her mail, her son Brian rushed down the stairs and said in a curious voice, " Hey Ma, Who was that? Chief Lambert was startled and answered back, " Rita from across the street. Brian looked confused, scratched his head, and replied, Lil Rita?

Chief Lambert started taking her shoes off, placed them in the closet, and answered back, " Yeah, Lil Rita got her driver's license today. Brian's eyes bucked wide open, and he shouted, " What? How old is she now? Chief Lambert replied, " Sixteen. Brian was in great surprise and went down memory lane, declaring, " Wow, I remember when Lil Rita was gathering her dolls having tea parties in the front yard.

Chief Lambert smiled, took a deep breath, whistled, and said

" Yeah. So son; What are you doing tonight? Brian sat on the couch looking out the window and replied," Nothing, probably check out the library and study, I have a test next week, and I need a couple more articles. Why? Chief Lambert nudged Brian and said," I thought you would want to go to bingo or catch a movie with your old mom.

Brian gave a funny expression, took a sip of his bottled water, and replied, "Mom, I'm twenty-seven years old; Bingo?! The last time you went to bingo, four older women argued because they forgot to say bingo after the fourth game; No, thank you! Chief Lambert had an unhappy look on her face and said, " Ok, son, Maybe next time. Brian kisses his mom on the cheek as she walks out of the room. He mumbles, " Yeah, next time. Brian is still looking out the window across the street at Lil Rita.

Chapter 8

STRATEGY IN CUE

Later that afternoon, detective Macy Pierce was feeling so anxious about getting to the investigation on these internet predators; as Macy finished her turkey sandwich, she dusted the bread crumbs off her hands and reached for her unlocked laptop and phone to call her new partner detective Naomi Barker. As Macy dials, she notices another site to add to her strategy; Naomi picks up the phone and says, " Hello. Macy dived right in with no hesitation and let out, " Hey Naomi, I logged in to the kiss after dark chat room, and it's a nerd gathering tonight. Wanna you go? Naomi quickly responded," You know I do. How many invites?

Macy clicked on the invite inbox and said, " Twenty invites but only ten accepted. Naomi was curious and asked, "Including you? An alert showed up, and Macy clicked on it and replied, " Yes. Naomi popped her bubble gum and asked Macy, " What time do you want me to be ready? Macy started to stretch her arms and said, "9:30 pm is fine. Naomi was distracted by a text message from her husband Stanley that read he's closing tonight and won't be home until 3 am. Macy took a deep breath, looked at the phone, and said," Naomi, Are you still there? Naomi snapped out of the zone and mumbled to Macy, " Sorry, I'm here. Ok, I'll meet you on West Grand Blvd in front of the mart with the blue light. Macy tells Naomi, " I'll be there, and Naomi get you some rest. Naomi yawned and answered, " I will. And they both hung up the phone.

Chapter 9

PICK YOUR POISON

A couple of hours later, Chief Lambert's son Brian was in his room blasting his music on his headphones, and eyes were on the computer typing fast; the clock read nine o'clock. Chief Lambert yelled up the steps," Leaving for bingo, son; see you when I get back! Brian turned his music off and replied," Alright, mom, be safe! Brian grabbed his books and started packing up his stuff for the gathering, his phone started to buzz, and it was one of his friends.

Brian answered and wiped the sweat from his forehead and said, "Look, man, I'll be there. My mom just cleared out, and I gotta get a ride to the spot. Brian's friend Hunter replied excitedly, "Hurry up, man! We got two new books that just walked in. Before Brian hung up his phone, he heard Hunter Conversing with the girls saying," Ladies, are you all ready to study? The phone clicked off.

As Brian was walking out the door to start strolling to the gathering, Brian listened to Lil Rita walking to her car, talking to her Big Mama, saying, " I'm just going to drop the videos off, I'll be right back. Soon as Lil Rita was bagging her car into the street, she adjusted the mirror and noticed Brian; Lil Rita rolled her window down to wave. Brian waved and said, "Hey Rita, How are you? Lil Rita started smiling and replied," I'm doing good; I got my new car.

Brian placed his hand on the top of the car and whispered " I see you got your license, Wow! Congratulations to you. Lil Rita gripped the steering wheel and said " Thank you! Do you need a ride? Brian fanned his hand and answered back " Naw, I'm straight. Lil Rita starts teasing Brian, making Chicken sounds, and says, " Whatcha scared? Brian adjusted his hat and reacted by saying, " Naw, never that sweetie.

Lil Rita gave Brian the eye and said, " Well, get in. Where do you want me to drop you off at? Brian got into the car and mumbled " West Grand Blvd.

Lil Rita rolled up her windows, So she could hear Brian and asked " Where? Brian repeated " West Grand blvd; It's a study gathering. Lil Rita felt lost and said" Study gathering? Whatcha studying? Brian paused and replied, " Uhh, anatomy, pull over to the right, and I can walk the rest of the way. Lil Rita laughed and said "Ok and anatomy that sounds interesting. Brian was looking at Rita's legs and started licking his lips.

Lil Rita pulled over and said " Alright Brian we're here. Brian replied, " Thank you" and tried to reach into his pocket to pay Lil Rita some money, and Lil Rita instantly responded, " No problem, Brian, you don't have to pay me. You looked out for me ever since I was a kid, Just returning a favor. Brian got out of the car, truly felt bad, and replied " Okay thanks a lot, Stay Safe Rita! Lil Rita shouted " Hey Brian! Could I check out the study party for a minute? Brian turned around and said " Just go home Rita, Big Mama is probably wondering where you are. Thanks, again! Lil Rita shook her head yes and answered back" Yeah, you're welcome. Brian walked to the house and Lil Rita pulled off.

Chapter 10

SURVEILLANCE SPEAKS

After Lil Rita drove off, she went to drop the videos off in the storage container down the street and noticed Brian forgot in the seat his study book; So she instantly turned the car around to return it. Brian was already in the house and saw food, beer bottles, and cups all over the floor. Brian's friend Hunter grabbed him from behind and shouted, "You're late, brother, and I'm horny as hell; I got three books that are ready to be unlocked!

Brian pushed Hunter off of him and said, " Man, I thought you weren't going to start until I got here. Let's get it accordingly. Lil Rita pulled up, grabbed Brian's study book, ran up to the door, and saw it wasn't closed all the way. Lil Rita knocked, and there was no answer, so she walked in and yelled for Brian and saw the room was in shambles; she noticed an opening that had colorful shingles dangling, and Lil Rita walked down the stairs and heard someone weeping as Lil Rita got closer to the bottom of the stairs she saw girls tied up and three men sexing them.

Lil Rita gasped, dropped Brian's book, and ran up the steps as she was running. A man snatched her into a dark room and tried to force himself on top of her. Lil Rita starts screaming for help and yelling for Brian. Another guy appeared, turned the music on, and tried to help the man calm Lil Rita down; shortly after, Lil Rita scratched the man's face, head-bumped the other dude, and began screaming for Brian.

Brian was in the room with a girl kissing, and just before he was going to remove her shirt, he had to go to the washroom because he smelled an odor under his armpit. Brian opened the bedroom door, walked down the hall, and heard loud music, banging on the door, and a girl yelling his name; Brian opened the door, flicked on the light, and there he saw

Lil Rita struggling to get away from the guys who were trying to force themselves on her. Brian shouted," Rita, What are you doing here! Outside were detectives Pierce and Barker, walking up to the front door undercover and ready to investigate their first internet investigation.

Soon as Brian turned the music off, Lil Rita started swinging a long sharp stick and screaming, crying out loud, " I can't believe you would do this to me, Brian! The guys were trying to grab the stick from her to calm her down. Detectives heard loud screaming and called for backup; they hustled into the house with their guns drawn, checked around, then burst into the room where they heard the chaos and saw Lil Rita in distress, and she fell unconscious.

One guy was shot in the hand as he was trying to reach for Lil Rita, and the other guy's neck was clasped and handcuffed. More authority arrived and checked everyone's license; Detective Macy Pierce noticed that one of the guys was Chief Lambert's son, Brian. The medical bus took Lil Rita and the other girls to check them out and the men to the police station to be booked and processed.

Chapter 11

GETTING READY TO BLOW

Detectives Pierce and Barker headed to the police station after contacting the young ladies' guardians and the tow truck service to pick up Lil Rita's vehicle. As they were driving, Macy talked to Naomi about the text message to Chief Lambert. Naomi was confused but kept quiet. Macy stopped at the red light and said, "Naomi, I want to apologize for my behavior at the beginning of meeting you; I said some horrible things to you out of irritation. Naomi turned to Macy with a tear in her eye and replied," I appreciate that, Macy. I wasn't as kind either, and I joined in with my pettiness.

Macy and Naomi start cracking up. Naomi said in an appreciative voice," I apologize to you as well, Macy, for entering your comfort space. Macy cut Naomi off and reacted," Listen, Sometimes when people are to assist, it's for a purpose, and I truly prayed for change, believe it or not. Naomi smiled and said jokingly," Wait, Don't tell me you're a holy rollie?! Macy pulled up to the police station and laughed and said," Holy Rollie? Girl, get out of my car! Naomi chuckled and said," I do have ice-cold beers now and then, but never on the job! Macy shook her head and said," Let's get in here and finish this task.

Naomi opened the station door for Macy and said," Alright, boss! The station called Chief Lambert in the middle of her bingo fun dressed in a colorful jacket with winning patches on the sleeves; Chief Lambert was strolling down the hallway towards Macy and Naomi. Macy smirked and said," Wow, Chief, never seen that attire before. Naomi raised her eyebrows and mumbled," Right.

Chief Lambert took her jacket off, cut the detectives off, and replied, "I just came from bingo, so you caught the internet freaks, huh! Good. Who are they?

Macy brought out her folder with notes and images that read " Issac Vaughn, Thomas Boi, Hunter Benjamin from Key West Florida, and Brian Lambert. Naomi chimed in and said," Thomas Boi is in Emergency; he got grazed in hand; We have one witness that could testify; her name is Sarita Heffman and Chief, her grandmother said she knows you. Chief Lambert was shocked at both names, realizing it could be her son Brian and neighbor, Lil Rita.

Chief Lambert, in a daze and declared," Wait a minute, Did you say, Brian Lambert? Macy looked at the notes and answered back in a low manner," Yes, I did, chief; why? Chief Lambert said in a denial way," No, you didn't say my son's name. Naomi was shocked and replied," Your son? Macy pulled out the image and extended it to Chief Lambert, and said," I'm sorry, Chief, Brian was in the house when we got in there. Naomi cuts Macy off and says," Brian says he didn't do anything; Rita dropped him off and left; Brian didn't know Rita came back.

Chief Lambert put her hand up with a disappointing look on her face and said," Let me have a minute to myself. Macy placed her hand on Chief Lambert's shoulder and said something to her. Chief snatched away hastily and shouted," I said let me have a Got damn minute Pierce to myself, please! Naomi pulled Macy and whispered," Come on, Macy. They walk away as Chief Lambert puts her head down and cries for a moment looking at her son's image, mumbling," Brian, why! After all, I do, and you do something like this; why? Chief Lambert shuts her office door and sits to gather her thoughts before speaking with her son.

Chapter 12

SPOILED ROTTEN

Meanwhile, in the police station, it was so chaotic. The phones were ringing nonstop, officials were booking and processing, and rude comments you could hear echoed down the hall. One of the guys, Issac Vaughn, secured from the internet freak gathering, shouted in a harsh voice," Man, I didn't do anything shit; where's my phone call? Detective Robyn Chase replied in a stern voice," Excuse me! Lower your tone, when it's time to make a phone call you will. Isaac clapped back and mumbled rudely " It betta be soon, I mean that shit!

Detective Chase raised her eyebrows and publicized " You all need to be processed then you could make your phone call, trust you won't be leaving anytime soon. Isaac smacked his lips mumbling to himself and replied " Bull Shit! I know one thing, I betta get my phone call.

Isaac sat down on the bench and a broader size guy sat next to him in the holding cell, intimidating him. The broader guy stared at Issac in a mean look and said " What's your name? Isaac strangely looked at him and moved to the other side of the room.

Chief Lambert entered the room with a disgusted look on her face to meet with her son; Brian instantly yelled in a loud tone " Mama, I didn't do anything! Chief Lambert turned the recorder off and shouted " Shut up boy! What the hell is wrong with you? Do you know you could get charged with ravishment, Abduction and put on the sex offenders list as a pedafiler, huh? Do you know that? And Lil Rita….

Brian jumped up and cut Chief Lambert off and passionately voiced " I'm None of those names Mama, Little Rita I wouldn't dare touch her, That's crazy! Chief Lambert was so upset she slammed her hand down on the table and yelled " Then why were you there son? Why around these types of guys, huh son? Why? I can't help you son… It's out of my hands; Brian you have to go through the same process as a criminal.

Brian began crying and replied" Mama I'm not a criminal.

Chief Lambert stepped close to Brian's face and said" Son, I want to believe you right now, but I"m so embarrassed; what about me; Did it ever flash through your mind that your mom is the Chief of authority? Huh, son. Little Rita is scared to death! Brian facepalmed and responded " I told Lil Rita to go home, It wasn't supposed to go down like that, this was supposed to be a gathering, I didn't know about the girls being tied up, I swear mama! Chief Lambert looks at Brian with glassy eyes and says in a stern voice " Well, you have to prove it. As Chief Lambert walked toward the door, Brian started crying out," Mama, Mama! Please believe me, I swear to you, mama, I didn't do anything! I swear! Brian says I swear it echoed down the hall as the door locked.

Chapter 13

LET'S BE CLEAR

Moments later, the police station went from chaos to stillness; The detectives were working on their paperwork and linking their statements for court dates. Naomi was chewing bubble gum fast because she was nervous about their first bust. Macy finished her final paragraph on what the hospital found and what the officers dust off at the gathering. Unfortunately, Lil Rita's fingerprint was on Brian Lambert's study book that she dropped downstairs in the house.

Naomi closed her laptop, leaned toward Macy, and said," Man, this is going to be complicated. Macy clenched her coat because it was getting a little chilly in the foyer and replied," Yeah, hopefully, Chief is alright. Naomi starts blowing bubbles with her gum as Macy notices Chief Lambert coming in their direction; Macy hits Naomi's foot to get her attention. Naomi popped her bubble and sat up straight in the chair as Chief Lambert walked by and motioned them to her office. The detectives looked at each other, and Chief Lambert whispered," I need to see you detectives in my office, please. Macy and Naomi slowly walked behind the Chief into her office and sat in the chair.

Macy said in a low voice, "I'm sorry, Chief.

Chief Lambert quickly cut Macy off and said," I want you two to prove that my son is innocent. Macy took a deep breath in shock and replied," But Chief, How? Naomi started chewing her bubble gum quickly while Chief Lambert stood up in Macy's face and said," Damn it, Pierce! Listen for once; my son said he didn't know that the girls were going to be tied up, Brian knew it was going to be a gathering; If Lil Rita says what she had seen, then my son will have to serve some time but only for being there. Where are the other girls? Naomi looked at her watch and answered back," They are still at the hospital; we have some quick notes from the girls.

Macy and Naomi said they would gather additional information to help prove Brian's innocence. Chief Lambert feels relieved that she has two of her best detectives on the assignment. Chief Lambert said she was going to speak with Lil Rita and her grandmother, but first, she wanted to apologize to Macy for blowing up at her when her son Brian's image and the name were called.

Macy accepted Chief Lambert's apology and wanted to speak with the Chief soon about the text messages Macy sent some months ago. Chief Lambert took a deep breath and said to the detectives she was about to take off and try to speak with Lil Rita's grandmother; she knows that she's upset about this whole thing. Naomi receives a text message from her husband Stanley saying he will be closing the bar tonight. Macy checks her watch, turns to Naomi, and asks if everything was alright? Naomi responded " I'm good. Stanley is shutting the bar down tonight.

Macy's cell phone rang. It was the hospital calling so Macy answered and put the phone on speaker. Macy says" Hello! On the other end, you can hear Lil Rita had just woken up screaming she wanted to talk to Brian. Chief Lambert and Naomi were listening in shock. The nurse says" Detective Pierce, I need someone to come to the clinic; Sarita Heffman is demanding to speak with Brian, and she doesn't want to talk to anyone else. Macy stared at Chief Lambert and whispered" What shall I do Chief? Chief Lambert replied" Tell the nurse you're on your way. Macy said to the nurse that she will be there in 15 minutes, The nurse said ok and hung up the phone.

Chief Lambert said" Ok detectives report back to me soon as you know something. Macy responded" Chief, Lil Rita only wants to speak with Brian. Chief Lambert replied " Detective Pierce, you of all people are the best to figure out this situation, Get down there and find out what will prove my son's innocence. Naomi chimes in " I'm going with you partner, Let's solve this case completely! Macy sighed and said " Alright, Let's go! Thanks, Chief. Chief Lambert placed her hand on her heart and said," Thank you, detectives, now go! Both detectives grabbed their stuff and waved goodbye.

Chapter 14

DOCUMENTATION BEATS CONVERSATION

Macy and Naomi rushed to their vehicle to head down to the medical center, feeling encouraged to get to the root of this internet bust. Naomi received another text message from her husband, Stanley stating he was not feeling too well and would see her at home. "Macy glanced at Naomi's expression and said," You okay? Naomi responded in a deep thought tone, "No. Since Stanley and I moved here, we haven't spent time together. Macy replied," Naomi, you don't have to come with me; I got this! I'm dropping you off at home.

Naomi turned to Macy and said, "Macy, You don't have to do that. We are a team. Macy swerved the car around and replied," Naomi, You can't work knowing your husband is feeling sick. Naomi smiled and said," Thanks, Partner! Macy grinned and uttered," No problem, Partner! Macy pulled into Naomi's driveway and noticed that all the lights were out and Stanley's vehicle wasn't there. Naomi grabbed her keys, played it cool while getting out of the car, and told Macy Thank you. Macy said, you're welcome and watched Naomi walk to the door. Macy starts hurrying to the medical center with many questions in her head for Lil Rita.

Back at Naomi's house, there were a lot of old papers spread on the coffee table; Naomi immediately called Her husband Stanley, but there was no answer. Moments later, Stanley walked into the house on the phone; Naomi turned on the lamp, stood up with the old papers collected in her hand, and asked Stanley," Why are my old documents out of my box? Stanley told the person on the phone that he would call them back. Naomi ran to the kitchen and grabbed a cold beer out of the fridge, and took a sip, while Stanley hurried behind her and snatched it away.

Stanley grabbed Naomi and said," Today marks the day we had our first child…I remember painting the nursery too early, and you got sick. Naomi tried to cut Stanley off, but he placed his hand over Naomi's mouth and continued to speak. Stanley said, "Every time around this month, I worry that you would leave me because of that day. Naomi wiped the tears from her eyes and hugged Stanley, and said," Honey, It's not your fault; I love you, and we will get through this. Stanley replied," Let's try again to have a baby; this time around goes straight by the books. Naomi smiled and said, "Let's take a moment to get it together in our current space. Stanley kissed Naomi's hand and said," Okay, I love you, and in 6 months, we are attempting to have a baby but if it happens before then, promise to embrace it stress-free. Naomi says with a nervous giggle," Okay, goodnight, honey! Stanley starts walking to the bedroom and turns around, and says to Naomi," No more drinking. Naomi replies," Okay, I hear you, and no more late-night grub. Stanley started walking away; mumbled under his breath," Deal.

Chapter 15

REMEMBER ME

Macy arrived at the Medical Center peeking through the sliding doors while walking towards the security desk. An unfashionable woman approached her and tapped Macy on the shoulder. The woman asked for some change for the vending machine to purchase a soda; Macy checked her back pocket to see if she had any change. The aged woman said to Macy that she looked familiar and asked if she was related to Penny Lynn. Macy gave the woman four quarters and said," No ma'am, I'm not. The aged woman looked flustered and said," Ok, thank you! Macy clasped her folder and walked away.

The security desk crowded with people asking questions, so Macy waited for a nurse to pass by and texted Naomi. The unfashionable woman sat next to Macy, munching on popcorn, she offered her to have some, but Macy told the aged woman no thank you. Macy saw that the security desk was clear, and she rushed to speak with the security; she dropped her folder, and a statement fell to the floor. The aged woman picked it up and read the paper and noticed her granddaughter's name on it; As Macy was walking towards the elevator, the unfashionable woman flagged Macy to return her report.

Macy walked into the elevator as the door was closing, and the unfashionable woman stuck her hand in the way; so the door wouldn't shut. The aged woman gave Macy the paper and stayed in the elevator. It was quiet for one second, and Macy turned to the woman and replied," Thank you! What floor? The aged woman answered back," The same floor you're going to; not to be rude, but I sensed something about you, I asked you if you knew Penny Lynn, and you said," No ma'am. Macy tried to cut the aged woman off, and the elevator sounded.

Macy walked out of the elevator towards the nurse's station, and the aged woman followed behind her; As Macy was walking to inquire about Sarita Hoffman, The nurse glanced from afar and saw the older woman. The nurse hung up the phone and came over to the unfashionable woman to let her know that Lil Rita was open-eyed and asking to see her now. Macy's eyes grew big, and she interrupted the nurse and asked the aged woman if she could visit Sarita with her? The aged woman looked at Macy and whispered, "No, Ma'am. Macy instantly pulled out her phone and texted Naomi, and the old woman tugged Macy by the arm and whispered," The only reason I'm allowing you in Sarita's room; is that you and your partner saved my grandbaby, and you were so kind to give me change for the vending machine.

Macy stared into the aged woman's eyes and said," I respect that, Mrs…. The old woman smiled and replied," Mrs. Lynn, but everyone calls me Big Mama. Macy glowed and responded," Thank you, Big Mama.

Chapter 16

MEMORY BANK

Later that evening, Chief Lambert finally left the station, pulled up into her driveway, and noticed a package on her porch. She made sure her weapon was on her hip; due to the high suspicion of her son being held without bail until someone validated his innocence. Chief Lambert grabbed her keys cell phone and prepared to check her surroundings as she strolled up to her porch. A car was driving up the block slow with jazz music playing loud. Chief Lambert turned around nervously and had her drop her keys.

Chief Lambert picked up her house keys, unlocked the door, and brought the package inside. As Chief Lambert was looking at the box to read the inscription, her phone beeped; it was a text message from Stanley, wanting to finish their discussion tomorrow morning because Naomi was home. Chief Lambert put her glasses on to read the package, and the phone beeped; It was a text from Macy letting her know she was at the hospital in the room with Mrs. Heffman, Sarita's grandma, and she will call in an hour.

Chief Lambert's eyes grew more prominent when she read Macy's text, glanced at the package, and realized it said, Penny Lynn. Chief Lambert opened up the box, unfolding the message inside that read, "The many times I've protected you, You left me! Chief Lambert cried out," This can't be happening to me! Chief Lambert finished opening the package, and it was a locket with a baby image in it, a newborn blanket with Lynn written in cursive.

Chief Lambert heard a loud sound outside and dropped the newborn blanket, and rushed to the window. The exact vehicle played the jazz music loudly and stopped in front of Chief Lambert's house, and got out of the car. It was a tall gentleman with a red cap with a dozen roses in his hands. Chief Lambert turned on her porch light to get a better look at who this man was walking lamely toward her steps. The gentleman rang the doorbell, and Chief Lambert asked, "Who it was?

The voice on the other side of the door said in a soft accent," Penny; It's Michael. Chief Lambert took a deep breath and asked," What do you want, Michael? Michael replied, "I want to talk to you. Chief Lambert hit the door with passion and shouted," After twenty-something years, Michael, you decide to find me! Then they mailed me a package with a name I don't go by anymore! And have the nerve to show up unannounced at my house with roses, kick rocks with no shoes on and return to your cave.

Michael placed the roses on the porch with an envelope attached that read My darling wife Penny Lynn and limped away with a pathetic look on his face. Chief Lambert watched Michael return to his vehicle from the window. Michael saw and blew her a kiss, took off his wedding ring, put it in the mailbox, jumped in his car, and left. Chief Lambert, with tears in her eyes, opened the front door, picked up a dozen roses from the porch, and slowly walked to her mailbox, got the ring out that Michael left. Chief Lambert went back into her house, fell to the floor, opened the envelope, and there was a long letter that read." Dear Beloved wife, Penny Lynn, I trust you're doing well. I don't know how to start this letter, but I foresee finishing it. I want to thank you for taking the time to read this letter; sorry it took so long; as you know, I've always been a man of short conversation. Not at this moment. This time, a young man reached out to me; I want to say, like a year ago today, while I was battling prostate cancer, he was looking for his father, and it linked to me. Penny, it's our son, and his name is Stanley Barker. He lived in Tennessee and now resides there in Detroit. I know that you don't want to see nor speak with me, and that's fine. I will be here for a couple of weeks to spend time with him. My mom has some more news that she's going to expose soon. I will be helping out at Country Ray's bar, where our son manages if you care to speak. I will always love you, even though we were so far apart! Love,

Michael Lynn P.S My beloved wife, Penny Lynn, The doctor says, I have one year to live. Chief Lambert finished the letter and laid on the floor holding the newborn blanket, with tears from her eyes, just weeping while her cell phone rang.

Chapter 17

UNCOVER IT

Meanwhile, at the Medical Center, Macy walked into Lil Rita's room with Mrs. Lynn. The nurse assisted Lil Rita to the restroom to shower before she laid back down for the night. Macy grouped text Chief Lambert and Naomi to let them know it's some odd stuff that's happening; Mrs. Lynn's purse dropped on the floor, as Macy reached down to pick it up, Mrs. Lynn noticed a locket around Macy's neck. The door unlocked, and Lil Rita cried out," Big Mama, where's Brian? He was trying to help me, and these ladies took him to jail! Lil Rita noticed Macy standing in the room against the wall and yelled, "What are you doing here? She's one of them!

Mrs. Lynn grabbed Lil Rita, and the nurse pleaded with Macy to leave the room until Lil Rita calmed down. Macy got her folder and went into the hallway; she dialed Chief Lambert's number, but there was no answer. Macy called Naomi, and there was no answer, so she called the police station to inquire if anyone had seen or heard from the Chief Since Earlier. Detective Robyn Chase answered the phone and provided Macy with more information that Brian was trying to help Sarita Heffman. The other young ladies said the guy from Florida invited them. They never saw a Brian, simply three men they could identify. Macy asked, "Detective Chase, How many young ladies were there total? Detective Chase replied," On the report, it states Four, The police officers took three to the medical center.

Macy's eyebrows lifted, and she took in a deep breath and said," Robyn can you do me a favor? Find out if Brian saw any girls besides Sarita, and whose house was it? Detective Robyn Chase typed in the address quickly and answered back," That's easy; the house is in a Rena Jones. I will text you back what Brian says about seeing other girls besides Sarita. Macy checked her phone for the time and replied," Ok, Robyn, thank you! Detective Robyn Chase told Macy," You're welcome.

As Macy ended the call, the nurse walked into the hallway and motioned Macy to come back into Lil Rita's room. Macy hurried in the room as Lil Rita moaned," Brian and mumbling." He only tried to save me, let him free! Macy took out her cell phone and requested Big Mama for consent to tape; Big Mama nodded yes. Voice recording of Lil Rita started. Big Mama was rubbing Lil Rita's hands and silently praying. Macy's text message beeped and popped up. "Brian is innocent. He was in the room with nineteen-year-old Rena Jones for only

ten minutes, but he went to the restroom because he was a little sour under the arms and gave attention to someone screaming his name. I hope that helps you, Detective Pierce.

Macy finished recording and read her text message; Big Mama said to Macy. " How well do you know the Chief? Macy placed her hands in her pocket and replied," almost seven years. The nurse came to give Lil Rita some pain medication in her I.V; Big Mama whispered to Lil Rita," Big Mama will be right back, precious. Let me speak to the detective for a moment. Macy finished recording Lil Rita's version of the story and added it to the case.

Big Mama focused again on the locket around Macy's neck and asked where she got it from? Macy squeezed her locket and said it was a family heirloom, and my aunt, who passed away, placed my baby picture inside it. Big Mama smiled and said," Your aunt was a remarkable woman. Macy mumbled Yes, she was. '' Macy cleared her throat and asked, "Big Mama, does she retain additional information about the case? Big Mama was mesmerized by how much Macy looked like her daughter Melanie, and she finally got a chance to share what she knew.

"Big Mama," asked if she could hug Macy? Macy responded in a confused posture and replied," Sure. As Big Mama was hugging Macy, the elevator door opened, and there was Big Mama's son Michael Lynn. Macy's phone buzzed, and it was a text from Chief Lambert wanting to know the progress on Proving Brian was innocent. Macy texted back, yes;

I will fill you in when I leave the Medical Center. Michael quickly walked over to Big Mama, hugged her, kissed her cheek, and asked how Lil Rita was doing? Macy told Big Mama that she needed to go and report back to Chief Lambert. Michael stared at Macy and said," Penny? Is your chief Penny? Macy replied," Yes, Chief Penny Lambert.

Big Mama cut in and said," Okay, Thanks again for helping our Little Rita. Macy replied," You're welcome; just simply fulfilling my job. Michael noticed Macy's locket and asked who gave it to her? Big Mama said," Her aunt gave it to her before she passed away. Macy mumbled", What is it about this locket? Michael said it's only a few like those. Big Mama's eyes start tearing up. Macy looked at Big Mama and asked if she was okay? Michael responded," No, she isn't. Big Mama sat down on the bench and motioned Macy to sit.

Michael placed his arm around Big mama and said, take a deep breath, mama, I'm here. Macy's eyes grew more prominent as Big Mama started to say that the locket Macy was wearing was her youngest daughter Melanie's and that Macy's father, Frank's oldest sister Rose gave it to Macy before she passed away. Frank Pierce was Big Mama's daughter Melanie Lynn's fiance.' She passed away, giving birth to Macy, and was removed from the Lynn family after

Melanie Lynn's funeral.

Macy was in disbelief and wanted to call her dad, but it was too late. Macy looked into Big Mama's eyes and said," You're my grandmother? Lil Rita is my cousin and Micheal, you're my uncle? Michael says," Yea, I know it's a lot to take in. And guess what? Your biological mom and Chief Lambert were good friends, but they met through your dad Frank; that's how you got into that job right after the field Academy. We've watched you grow and never got a chance to confirm it until my son reached out to me. Macy paused and said," Who is your son? Michael replied," Stanley Barker. Macy's phone was buzzing. She had to leave. It was Naomi; Macy grabbed her folder and hugged Big Mama, gave her card to Michael, and said she would talk to them both real soon.

Chapter 18

BAR RULES

After midnight, Macy headed to Bernie Ray's Country bar, hoping she would run into Stanley. Instead, she realizes Chief Lambert is sitting at the bar with dark shades. Macy walked over to the bar, and before Macy opened her mouth, Naomi grabbed Macy from behind. She explained that Stanley had told her the whole story that Chief Lambert is his mom and that his dad Michael only had a year to live, and that Macy's mom had the same family heirloom locket as all of the grandkids. Michael walks into the bar and joins Chief Lambert. Naomi and Macy sat in a booth in the back of the bar to observe.

Stanley texts Naomi that he will be meeting his dad Michael at the bar, and he wants her to meet him eventually. Macy opened her folder and shared with Naomi the information that confirmed Brian's innocence. Stanley walks into the bar, acknowledges Naomi and is surprised to see Macy, and says," And we meet again; How are you, Detective Pierce? Macy smiled and replied," Nice to see you again, cousin! Strange huh?

Stanley said," We have so much to catch up on; wait for me to signal you both over after I speak to my long-lost mother. Naomi chimed in and said," We have some Good news, beau, your half-brother is innocent, and since we are here at the bar, we can all celebrate. Stanley whistles for the waitress to bring a round of beers, and Naomi places her hand on her belly and "says," I reckon I have water; we wouldn't want our baby to be intoxicated so prematurely. Stanley and Macy looked at Naomi and said simultaneously," Are you joking?

Naomi pulled Stanley close to her, gave him a great big kiss, and whispered," Stanley Barker, you are going to be a Papa, suga. Stanley jumped on the chair and yelled," Attention everybody, I'm going to be a father! The whole bar cheered and clapped. ``Congratulations; Macy raised her water glass, smiled, and said," Now that's another reason to celebrate!